Robert Root

Andreas: the legend of St. Andrew

Translated from the Old English by Robert Kilburn Root

Robert Root

Andreas: the legend of St. Andrew
Translated from the Old English by Robert Kilburn Root

ISBN/EAN: 9783337150136

Printed in Europe, USA, Canada, Australia, Japan

Cover: Foto ©Andreas Hilbeck / pixelio.de

More available books at **www.hansebooks.com**

YALE STUDIES IN ENGLISH

ALBERT S. COOK, Editor

VII

ANDREAS:

THE LEGEND OF ST. ANDREW

TRANSLATED FROM THE OLD ENGLISH

BY

ROBERT KILBURN ROOT

NEW YORK
HENRY HOLT AND COMPANY
1899

ERRATA.

p. IV.   For *Angelsächsen* read *Angelsachsen.*

p. V.   "   Fritsche   "   Fritzsche.

p. IX.   "   homilest   "   homilist.

p. 18, l. 550. "   has   "   hast.

p. 27, l. 835. "   'Till   "   Till.

p. 57.   "   Siever's   "   Sievers'.

PREFACE

It is always a somewhat hardy undertaking to attempt the translation of poetry, for such a translation will at the best be but a shadow of that which it would fain represent. Yet I trust that even an imperfect rendering of one of the best of the Old English poems will in some measure contribute towards a wider appreciation of our earliest literature, for the poem is accessible to the general reader only in the baldly literal and somewhat inaccurate translation of Kemble, published in 1843, and now out of print.

I have chosen blank verse as the most suitable metre for the translation of a long and dignified narrative poem, as the metre which can most nearly reproduce the strength, the nobility, the variety and rapidity of the original. The ballad measure as used by Lumsden in his translation of *Beowulf* is monotonous and trivial, while the measure used by Morris and others, and intended as an imitation of the Old English alliterative measure, is wholly impracticable. It is a hybrid product, neither Old English nor modern, producing both weariness and disgust; for, while copying the external features of its original, it loses wholly its æsthetic qualities.

In my diction I have sought after simple and idiomatic English, studying the noble archaism of the King James Bible, rather than affecting the Wardour Street dialect of William Morris or Professor Earle, which is often utterly unintelligible to any but the special student of Middle English. My translation is faithful, but not literal; I have not hesitated to make a passive construction active, or to translate a compound adjective by a phrase. To quote from King Alfred's preface to his translation of Boethius, I have "at times translated word by word, and at times sense by sense, in whatsoever way I might most clearly and intelligibly interpret it."

The text followed is that of Grein-Wülker in the *Bibliothek der Angelsächsischen Poesie* (Leipzig, 1894), and the lines of my translation are numbered according to that edition. I have not, however, felt obliged to follow his punctuation. Where it has seemed best to adopt other readings, I have mentioned the fact in my notes.

I have compared my translation with those of Kemble and Grein *(Dichtungen der Angelsächsen)*, and am occasionally indebted to them for a word or a phrase.

It gives me great pleasure to acknowledge my indebtedness to Dr. Frank H. Chase, who has very carefully read my translation in manuscript ; and to Professor Albert S. Cook, who has given me his help and advice at all stages of my work from its inception to its publication. To Mr. Charles G. Osgood, Jr., I am also indebted for valuable criticism.

ROBERT KILBURN ROOT.

YALE UNIVERSITY,
April 7, 1899.

INTRODUCTION

The Manuscript. While traveling in Italy during the year 1832, Dr. Blume, a German scholar, discovered in the cathedral library at Vercelli an Old English manuscript containing both poetry and prose. The longest and the best of the poems is the *Andreas*, or *Legend of St. Andrew*.

How did this manuscript find its way across the Alps into a country where its language was wholly unintelligible? Several theories have been advanced, the most plausible being that advocated by Cook.[1] According to this view it was carried thither by Cardinal Guala, who during the reign of Henry III was prior of St. Andrew's, Chester. On his return to Italy he built the monastery of St. Andrew in Vercelli, strongly English in its architecture. Since the manuscript contained a poem about St. Andrew, it would have been an appropriate gift to St. Andrew's Church in Vercelli. Wülker's theory that it was owned by an Anglo-Saxon hospice at Vercelli rests on very shadowy arguments, since he adduces no satisfactory proof that such a hospice ever existed.

Authorship and Date. On the strength of certain marked similarities of style and diction to the signed poems of Cynewulf, the earlier editors of the *Andreas* assigned the poem to him, and were followed by Dietrich, Grein, and Ten Brink. But Fritsche (*Anglia* II), arguing from other equally marked dissimi-

---

[1] *Cardinal Guala and the Vercelli Book*, Univ. of Cal. Library Bulletin No. 10. Sacramento, 1888.

larities, denies its Cynewulfian authorship, and is sustained in his position by Sievers, though vigorously opposed by Ramhorst. More recently Trautman (*Anglia*, Beiblatt VI. 17) reasserts the older view, declaring his belief that the *Fates of the Apostles*, in which Napier has discovered the runic signature of Cynewulf, is but the closing section of the *Andreas*. There is much to be said in favor of this last theory, which would establish Cynewulf as the author of the entire work ; but the whole question is far from being settled. We can at least affirm that the author was a devout churchman and a dweller by the sea, thoroughly acquainted with the poems of Cynewulf.

It is equally impossible to determine with any certainty the date of authorship, since the poem is wholly lacking in contemporary allusions. Nor can we base any argument upon its language, since, in all probability, its present form is but a West Saxon transcript of an older Northumbrian or Mercian version. If Cynewulf flourished in the eighth century, the date of the *Andreas* is probably not much later. The Vercelli manuscript is assigned to the first half of the eleventh century.

Sources. Fortunately we can speak with more assurance about the sources of the poem. It follows closely, though not slavishly, the *Acts of Andrew and Matthew*, contained in the *Apocryphal Acts of the Apostles.*[1] Like the great English poets of the fourteenth and sixteenth centuries, the poet of the *Andreas* has borrowed his story from a foreign source, and like them he has added and altered until he has made it thoroughly his own and thoroughly English. We can learn from it the tastes and

[1] *Acta Apostolorum Apocrypha*, ed. Tischendorf. Leipzig, 1851, pp. 132-166. (For a translation of part of the *Acts of Andrew and Matthew*, see Cook's *First Book in Old English*, Appendix III.)

ideals of our Anglo-Saxon forefathers quite as well as from a poem wholly original in its composition. Most clearly do we discover their love of the sea. The action of the story brings in a voyage, which the Greek narrative dismisses with a few words, merely as a piece of necessary machinery. The Old English poem, on the contrary, expands the incident into many lines. A storm is introduced and described with great vigor ; we see the circling gull and the darting horn-fish ; we hear the creaking of the ropes and the roaring of the waves.[1] Every mention of the sea is dwelt upon with lingering affection, and described with vivid metaphor. It is now the "bosom of the flood," now the "whale-road" or the "fish's bath." Again it is the "welter of the waves," or its more angry mood is personified as the "Terror of the waters." In the first 500 lines alone there are no less than 43 different words and phrases denoting the sea.

Daybreak and sunset, too, are described with much beauty, and in one passage at least with strong imagination. We can have no doubt that the poet was a close watcher and keen lover of nature. We can imagine him walking on the cliffs beside his beloved ocean, watching for the sunrise, rejoicing in the glory of the sky,

As heaven's candle shone across the floods.[2]

I have said, too, that he was a devout churchman. Many of the noble hymns and prayers with which the poem abounds are largely original, expanded from a mere line or two in the Greek. Many and beautiful are the epithets or kennings which he applies to God, taken in part from the Bible, and in part from the imagery of the not wholly extinct heathen mythology.

[1] See 369–381.   [2] See 243.

Thoroughly English is his love of violent action, of war and bloodshed. Andrew is a "warrior brave in the battle"; the apostles are

> Thanes of the Lord, whose courage for the fight
> Failed never, e'en when helmets crashed in war,

and their missions are rather military expeditions than peaceful pilgrimages.

One concrete example will serve well to show in what spirit the author has dealt with his original. The disciples of Andrew are so terrified by the sea that the Lord (disguised as a shipmaster) suggests that they shall go ashore and await the return of their master. In the Greek the disciples answer: "If we leave thee, then shall we be strangers to those good things which the Lord hath promised unto us. Therefore will we abide with thee, wherever thou go."[1] In the Old English :—

> O whither shall we turn us, lordless men,
> Mourning in heart, forsaken quite by God,
> Wounded with sin, if we abandon thee?
> We shall be odious in every land,
> Hated of every folk, when sons of men,
> Courageous warriors, in council sit,
> And question which of them did best stand by
> His lord in battle, when the hand and shield,
> Worn out by broadswords on the battle-plain,
> Suffered sore danger in the sport of war. (405-414.)

There is in the Greek no trace of the Teutonic idea of loyalty to a lord, which is the ruling motive of the Old English lines.

But did the poet read the legend in the Greek? The study of that language had, it is true, been introduced into England in the seventh century by Archbishop Theodore[1],

---

[1] Bede, *Hist. Eccl.* IV. 2.

but we can hardly assume that this study was very general. Moreover, there are several important variations between the poem and the *Acts of Andrew and Matthew*, facts wanting in the Greek, which the poet could not possibly have invented. For example, the poem states that Andrew was in Achaia when he received the mission to Mermedonia. In the Greek we find no mention of Achaia, nor is the name "Mermedonia" given at all. After the conversion of the Mermedonians, the poet says that Andrew appointed a bishop over them, whose name was Platan. Again the Greek is silent. There is, however, an Old English homily[1] of unknown authorship and uncertain date, which contains these three facts, (though the name of the bishop is not given). Still another remarkable coincidence has been pointed out by Zupitza.[2] In line 1189 of the *Andreas*, Satan is addressed as *dēofles strǣl* ("shaft of the devil "), and in the homily also the same word (*strǣl*) is found. But in the corresponding passage of the Greek we find 'Ω Βελία ἐχθρότατε ("O most hateful Belial "). From this correspondence between the poem and the homily, Zupitza argues the existence of a Latin translation of the Greek, from which both the *Andreas* and the homily were made, assuming that the ignorant Latinist confused Βελία (Belial) with Βέλος ("arrow," "shaft,"), translating it by *telum* or *sagitta*. It is hardly probable that both the poet and the homilest should have made the same mistake.

The homily could not have been drawn from the poem, nor the poem from the homily, for in each we find facts and phrases of the Greek not contained in the other. For example, both in the Greek and in the homily, the flood which sweeps away the Mermedonians proceeds from the

---

[1] Bright, *Anglo-Saxon Reader*, pp. 113–128.
[2] *Zeitschrift für Deutsches Altertum*, XXX. 175.

mouth of an alabaster image standing upon a pillar, while in the poem it springs forth from the base of the pillar itself. On the other hand, most of the dialogue between Andrew and the Lord on shipboard, as well as other important incidents, are wanting in the homily.

Summing up, then, we have the homily and the poem agreeing in some important points in which both differ from the Greek, but so dissimilar in other points that neither could have been the source of the other. In the light of these similarities and variations, and of others which space prevents me from mentioning, we must suppose the homily to have been taken from an abridgment of the Latin version, of which the poet saw a somewhat corrupt copy. It is also not improbable that this Latin version may have been made from a Greek manuscript varying in some details from the legend as it appears in Tischendorf's edition. This view is sustained by a Syrian translation, which in some respects agrees with our hypothetical Latin version. But this Latin version has never been discovered, though some fragments of the legend are found in the Latin of Pseudo-Abdias and the *Legenda Aurea*,[1] which curiously enough supply several of the facts missing in the Greek, namely, that Andrew was teaching in Achaia, and that the land of the Anthropophagi was called Mermedonia.

So much for the sources of the poem as a whole. The poet is also deeply indebted to the *Beowulf* and to the poems of Cynewulf (unless he be Cynewulf himself) for lines and phrases throughout his work. One example of this borrowing will suffice. In line 999, when Andrew reaches the prison, we read (translating literally): "The door quickly opened at the touch of the holy saint's hand."

[1] Grimm, *Andreas und Elene*, XIII–XVI.

In the Greek : "And he made the sign of the cross upon
the door, and it opened of its own accord." Why has the
poet omitted the sign of the cross? We are unable to
answer until we read in the *Beowulf* (721) that at the coming of the monster Grendel to Heorot " the door quickly
opened . . . . soon as he touched it with his hands."

The Poem as a
Work of Art.

How shall we rank the *Legend of St.
Andrew* among the other poems of the
Anglo-Saxons? and what are its chief
merits as a work of art? The Old English epics may be
divided into two general classes : the heroic epic, of which
the *Beowulf* is the chief example ; and the larger group
of religious epics, including the poems of Cynewulf, of
Pseudo-Cædmon, the *Judith*, and the *Andreas*.

In spite of occasional Christian interpolations the *Beowulf* is essentially pagan, the expression of English sentiments and ideals before Augustine led his little band of
chanting monks through the streets of Canterbury. In
the *Andreas* we see better, perhaps, than in any of the
religious epics, these same sentiments and ideals softened
and ennobled by the sweet spirit of the Christian religion.
We see the conversion of England in the very process of
its accomplishment. We see the beauties of Paganism and
those of Christianity blending with each other, much as the
Medieval and the Renaissance are blended in Spenser. In
the one aspect Andrew is the valiant hero, like Beowulf,
crossing the sea to accomplish a mighty deed of deliverance;
in the other he is the saintly confessor, the patient sufferer,
whose whole trust is in the Lord.

If we compare the poem with the other epics of its class,
its most formidable competitors are the anonymous *Judith*
and Cynewulf's *Christ*. But *Judith*, though unquestionably

more brilliant, is but a fragment of 350 lines, and the *Christ*, in spite of its many beautiful passages, is entirely lacking in movement. The *Andreas* is complete, and, if we except the long dialogue of Andrew and the Lord at sea, moves steadily towards the end with considerable variety of action. If the characterization is crude, the descriptions are vivid, the speeches are often vigorous, and the treatment of nature is throughout charming. It seems to me eminently suited by its subject and manner to stand as an example of the Old English religious epic, an example of a form of literature with which every serious student of our English poetry should be familiar. For English literature does not begin with Chaucer. He who would understand it well must know it also in its purer English form before the coming of the Normans.

The Argument. It only remains to give a brief synopsis of the poem. It has fallen to the lot of Matthew to preach the Gospel to the cannibal Mermedonians ; they seize him and his company, binding him and casting him into prison, where he is to remain until his turn comes to be eaten (1–58). He prays to God for help, and the Lord sends Andrew to deliver him (59–234). Andrew and his disciples come to the seashore and find a bark with three seamen, who are in reality the Lord and His two angels. On learning that Andrew is a follower of Jesus, the shipmaster agrees to carry him to Mermedonia (234–359). A storm arises, at which the disciples of Andrew are greatly terrified ; he reminds them how Christ stilled the tempest, and they fall asleep (360–464). A dialogue ensues, in which Andrew relates to the shipmaster many of Christ's miracles (465–817). He falls asleep, and is carried by the angels to

Mermedonia. On awaking, he beholds the city, and his disciples sleeping beside him. They relate to him a vision which they had seen. The Lord appears and bids him enter the city, covering him with a cloud (818–989). He reaches the prison, the doors of which fly open at his touch, and rescues Matthew, whom he sends away with all his company (990–1057). The Mermedonians, confronted with famine, choose one of their number by lot to serve as food for the rest. He offers his son as a substitute, but, as the heathen are about to slay their victim, Andrew interposes and causes their weapons to melt away like wax (1058–1154). Instigated by the Devil, they seize Andrew, and for three days subject him to the most cruel torments (1155–1462). On the fourth the Lord comes to his prison and heals him of his wounds. Beside the prison wall Andrew sees a marble pillar, which, at his command, sends forth a great flood, destroying many of the people (1462–1575). Andrew takes pity upon them and causes the flood to cease. The mountain is cleft and swallows up the waters, together with fourteen of the worst of the heathen. The others are restored to life and baptized. After building a church and appointing a bishop, Andrew returns to Achaia, followed by the prayers of his new converts (1575–1722).

THE LEGEND OF ST. ANDREW

Lo! we have learned of Twelve in days gone by,
Who dwelt beneath the stars, in glory rich,
Thanes of the Lord, whose courage for the fight
Failed never, e'en when helmets crashed in war,
From that time when they portioned each his place,
As God himself declared to them by lot,
High King of heaven above. Renownèd men
Were they through all the earth, and leaders bold,
Brave in the battle, warriors of might,
When shield and hand the helmet did protect   10
Upon the field of fate. Of that brave band
Was Matthew one, who first among the Jews
Began to write the Gospel down in words
With wondrous power. To him did Holy God
Assign his lot upon that distant isle
Where never yet could any outland man
Enjoy a happy life or find a home.
Him did the murderous hands of bloody men
Upon the field of battle oft oppress
Right grievously. That country all about,
The folkstead of the men, was compassèd
With slaughter and with foemen's treachery,   20
That home of heroes. Dwellers in that land
Had neither bread nor water to enjoy,

I

But on the flesh and blood of stranger men,
Come from afar, that people made their feast.
This was their custom : every foreigner
Who visited that island from without
They seized as food—these famine-stricken men.
This was the cruel practice of that folk,
Mighty in wickedness, most savage foes :   30
With javelin points they poured upon the ground
The jewel of the head, the eyes' clear sight ;
And after brewed for them a bitter draught—
These wizards by their magic—drink accursed,
Which led astray the wits of hapless men,
The heart within their breasts, until they grieved
No longer for the happiness of men ;
Weary for food they fed on hay and grass.

When to this far-famed city Matthew came,   40
There rose great outcry through the sinful tribe,
That cursed throng of Mermedonians.
Soon as those servants of the Devil learned
The noble saint was come unto their land,
They marched against him, armed with javelins ;
Under their linden-shields they went in haste,
Grim bearers of the lance, to meet the foe.
They bound his hands ; with foeman's cunning skill
They made them fast—those warriors doomed to hell— 50
With swords they pierced the jewel of his head.
Yet in his heart he honored Heaven's King,
Though of the drink envenomed he had drunk,
Of virtue terrible ; steadfast and glad,
With courage unabashed, he worshiped still
The Prince of glory, King of heaven above ;
And from the prison rose his holy voice.

Within his noble breast the praise of Christ
Stood fast imprinted; weeping tears of woe,
With sorrowful voice of mourning he addressed
His Lord victorious, speaking thus in words :—
"Behold how these fierce strangers knit for me
A chain of mischief, an ensnaring net.
Ever have I been zealous in my heart
To do Thy will in all things; now in grief
The life of the dumb cattle I must lead.
Thou, Lord, alone, Creator of mankind,
Dost know the hidden thoughts of every heart.
O Prince of glory, if it be thy will—
That with the sword's keen edge perfidious men
Put me at rest, I am prepared straightway
To suffer whatsoever Thou, my Lord,
Who givest bliss to that high angel-band,
Shalt send me as my portion in this world,
A homeless wanderer, O Lord of hosts.
In mercy grant to me, Almighty God,
Light in this life, lest, blinded in this town
By hostile swords, I needs must longer bear
Reviling words, the grievous calumny
Of slaughter-greedy men, of hated foes.
On Thee alone, Protector of the world,
I fix my mind, my heart's unfailing love ;
So, Father of the angels, Lord of hosts,
Bright Giver of all bliss, to Thee I pray,
That Thou appoint me not among my foes,
Artificers of wrong forever damned,
The death most grievous on this earth of Thine."

After these words there came to his dark cell
A sacred sign all-glorious from heaven,

3

Like to the shining sun ; then was it shown   90
That holy God was working aid for him.
The voice of Heaven's Majesty was heard,
The music of the glorious Lord's sweet words,
Wondrous beneath the skies.   To His true thane
Brave in the fight, in dungeon harsh confined,
He promised help and comfort with clear voice :
" Matthew, My peace on earth I give to thee ;
Let not thy heart be troubled, neither mourn
Too much in mind ; I will abide with thee,
And I will loose thee from these bonds that bind   100
Thy limbs, and loose all that great multitude
That dwells with thee in strait captivity.
To thee I open by My holy power
The meadow radiant of Paradise,
Brightest of splendors, dwelling-place most fair,
That home most blessèd, where thou mayst enjoy
Glory and bliss to everlasting life.
Suffer this people's cruelty ; not long
Can faithless men afflict thee sinfully
With chains of torment by their crafty wiles.
Straight will I send unto this heathen town   110
Andrew to be thy comfort and defense ;
He will release thee from thine enemies.
Thou hast not long to wait ; in very truth
But seven and twenty days fulfil the time,
When, sorrow-laden, thou shalt go from hence,
Under God's care, with victory adorned."
The Holy One, Defense of all mankind,
The angels' Lord, departed to the land
High in the heavens—He is the King by right,   120
Steadfast He rules supreme in all the world.

Added)

Exalted high was Matthew at the voice
New-heard. The veil of darkness slipped away,
Vanished in haste ; and straightway came the light,
The murmuring sound of early reddening dawn.
The host assembled ; heathen warriors
Thronged in great crowds ; their battle-armor sang ;
Their spears they brandished, angry in their hearts,
Under the roof of shields ; they fain would see
Whether those hapless men were yet alive,
Who fast in chains within their prison-walls   130
Had dwelt a while in comfortless abode,
And which one they might first for their repast
Rob of his life after the time ordained.
They had set down, those slaughter-greedy foes,
In runic characters and numerals
The death-day of those men, when they should serve
As food unto that famine-stricken tribe.
Then clamored loudly that cold-hearted brood ;
Throng pressed on throng ; their cruel counsellors
Recked not at all of mercy or of right.
Oft did their souls, led by the devil's lore,   140
Under the dusky shadows penetrate,
When in the might of beings ever-cursed
They put their trust. They found that holy man,
Prudent of mind, within his prison dark,
Awaiting bravely what the radiant King,
Creator of the angels, should vouchsafe.
Then was accomplished, all except three nights,
The appointed time, the season foreordained,
Which those fierce wolves of war had written down,
At end of which they planned to break his bones,   150
And, parting straight his body and his soul,
To portion out as food to old and young

5

The body of the slain, a welcome feast;
They cared not for the soul, those greedy men,
How after death the spirit's pilgrimage
Might be decreed. So every thirty nights
They held their feast; most fierce was their desire
To tear with bloody jaws the flesh of men   160
To be their food. Then He, who with strong might
Stablished this world, was mindful how that saint
Abode in misery 'mongst stranger men,
Fast bound in chains—that saint who for His sake
Had suffered from the Hebrews, had withstood
The magic incantations of the Jews.

   Where in Achaia holy Andrew dwelt,
Guiding his people in the way of life,   170
A voice was heard from out the heavens above.
To him, that steadfast saint, the Lord of hosts,
Glory of kings, Creator of mankind,
Unlocked the treasure of His heart, and thus
In words He spake:—" Thou shalt go forth and bear
My peace, and journeying shalt fare where men,
Devourers of their kind, possess the land,
And hold their home secure by murderous might.
This is the custom of that multitude:
Within their land they spare no stranger's life,
But when those evil-doers chance to find
A helpless wight in Mermedonia,   180
Death must be dealt and cruel murder done.
I know that 'mongst those townsmen, fast in chains,
Thy brother dwells, that saint victorious.
It lacks but three nights of the time ordained,
When, midst that people, by the hard-gripped spear,
In struggle with the heathens, he must needs

Send forth his soul all ready to depart ;
Unless thou come before the appointed time."

Straightway did Andrew answer him again :
" My Lord, how can I o'er the ocean deep   190
My course accomplish, to that distant shore,
As speedily as Thou, O King of glory,
Creator of the heavens, dost command ?
That road thine angel can more easily
Traverse from heaven ; he knows the watery ways,
The salt sea-streams, the wide path of the swan,
The battle of the surf against the shore,
The terror of the waters, and the tracks
Across the boundless land. These foreign men
Are not my trusty friends, nor do I know
In any wise the counsels of this folk ;   200
To me the cold sea-highways are unknown."

Him answered then the everliving Lord :—
" Alas, O Andrew, that thou shouldst be slow
To undertake this journey, since for God,
Almighty One, it were not hard to bring
That city hither, 'neath the circling sun,
Unto this country, o'er the ways of earth—
The princely city famous, with its men—
If He, the Lord of Glory, with a word   210
Should bid it. So thou mayst not hesitate
To undertake this journey, nor art thou
Too weak in wit, if thou but keepest well
The faithful covenant with thy Lord. Be thou
Prepared against the hour, for there can be
No tarrying on this errand. Thou shalt go
And bear thy life into the grasp of men

7

Full violent, where 'gainst thee shall be raised
The strife of warfare, with the battle-din
Of heathens, and the warriors' martial might.
Even to-morrow with the early dawn,   220
At the sea's border thou shalt straightway go
On shipboard, and upon the waters cold,
Over the ocean¹, break thy speedy way.
Thou hast My blessing over all the earth,
Wherever thou shalt fare!"   The Holy One,
Ruler and Guardian, archangels' King,
The world's Defense, betook Him to His home,
That glorious home, where souls of righteous men
After the body's fall shall life enjoy.
So in that town this mission was decreed   230
Unto the noble champion ; not abashed
In mind was he, but steadfast for the deed
Heroic ; hardy-hearted, firm in soul,
No skulker he from battle, but prepared
For warfare, in God's struggle stout and bold.

So at the dawning, when the day first broke,
He gat him o'er the sand-downs to the sea,
Valiant in heart, and with him went his thanes
To walk upon the shingle, where the waves
Loud thundered, and the streams of ocean beat
Against the shore.   Full glad was that brave saint
To see upon the sands a galley fair   240
Wide-bosomed.   Then, behold, resplendent dawn,
Brightest of beacons, came upon her way,
Hasting from out the murky gloom of night,
And heaven's candle shone across the floods.
Three seamen saw he there, a glorious band,

¹ Lit. "bath-road."

Courageous men, upon their ocean-bark
Sitting all ready to depart, like men
Just come across the deep. The Lord himself
It was, the everlasting Lord of hosts,
Almighty, with His holy angels twain.
In raiment they were like seafaring men,   250
These heroes, like to wanderers on the waves,
When in the flood's embrace they sail with ships
Upon the waters cold to distant lands.

Then he who stood there, eager, on the shore,
Upon the shingle, greeted him and said :—
" Whence come ye, men in seamanship expert,
Seafaring on your ocean-coursing bark,
Your lonely ship? whence has the ocean-stream
Wafted you o'er the welter of the waves?"

Then answered him again Almighty God,   260
In such wise that the saint who heard His words
Wist not what one of speaking men it was
With whom he was conversing on the strand.
" From the land of Mermedonia are we come,
Borne hither from afar ; our high-prowed ship
Carried us o'er the whale's road with the flood,
Our sea-horse fleet, all girt about with speed,
Until we reached the country of this folk,
Sea-beaten, as the wind did drive us on."

Then Andrew humbly answered him again :—   270
" I fain would beg thee, though but little store
Of jewels or of treasure I can give,
That thou wouldst bring us in thy lofty ship,
Over the ocean' on thy high-beaked boat,

¹ Lit. "whale's home."

9

Unto that people; thou shalt meed receive
From God, if kindness thou but show to us
Upon our journey."

The Defense of kings,
Maker of angels, answered from His ship :—
" Wide-faring foreigners can never dwell
There in that country, nor enjoy the land ;   280
But in that city they must suffer death
Who thither bring their lives from distant shores.
And dost thou wish to traverse the wide main,
That thou mayst spill thy life in bitter war ?"

To him did Andrew answer give again :—
" Our hearts' strong hope and yearning drives us forth
To seek that country and that far-famed town,
If thou, most noble sir, wilt show to us
Thy gracious kindness on the wave-tossed deep."

Then from His vessel's prow, the angels' Lord,   290
The Savior of mankind, replied to him :—
" Gladly and freely we will carry thee
Across the ocean[1], e'en to that far land
Which thy desire doth urge thee so to seek,
When thou shalt give us the accustomed sum,
Thy passage-money ; so upon our bark
We seamen will grant honor unto you."

Then straightway Andrew spake to him in words,
That friendless saint :—" I have no beaten gold,   300
No treasures, neither wealth nor sustenance,
No golden clasps, no land, nor bracelets woven,

[1] Lit. "fish's bath."

That thy desire I now may satisfy,
Thy worldly wishes, as thou sayst in words."
The Prince of Men gave answer where He sat
Upon the gangway, o'er the dashing surge :—
" How comes it thou wouldst visit, my dear friend,
The sea-hills, boundaries of the ocean-streams,
To seek a vessel by the cold sea-cliffs   310
All penniless? Hast thou no store of bread
To comfort thee upon the ocean-road,
Or pure drink for thy thirst? The life is hard
For him who journeys far upon the flood."

     In answer then did Andrew, wise in wit,
Unlock to him the treasure of his words :—
" It is not seemly that with arrogance
And words of taunting thou demand reply,
When God hath given thee abundant wealth
And worldly fortune ; better for each man   320
That with humility he kindly greet
A traveler bound to other lands far off,
As Christ commanded, Lord most glorious.
We are His thanes, chosen as champions ;
He is the King by right, Author and Lord
Of wondrous glory, one eternal God
Of all created things ; by His sole might
He comprehendeth all the heavens and earth
With holy strength, Giver of victory.
He spake the word himself, and bade us fare   330
Throughout the spacious earth, converting souls :—
'Go now to all the corners of the earth,
Far as the waters compass it about,
Far as the meadows lie along the roads,
And preach the glorious Faith throughout the towns

Upon earth's bosom ; I am your defense.
No gold nor silver treasures need ye bear
Upon this journey. I will freely give
All things that ye may need.' Lo, thou thyself
Mayst hear the story of our journeying   340
With thoughtful mind. Right quickly shall I learn
What kindness thou wilt show us on our way."

   The Lord eternal answered him again :—
" If ye are thanes of Him who did exalt
His glory o'er the world, as ye declare,
And ye have kept the Holy One's commands,
I'll gladly bear you o'er the ocean-streams,
As ye do beg me."

              Then upon the bark
They went, bold, valiant men ; the heart of each   350
Was filled with joy upon the tossing main.
Then Andrew, on the rolling of the waves,
Begged for that seaman mercy from the King
Who rules in glory; thus he spake in words :—
" May God, the Lord of men, give unto thee
Exceeding honor—happiness on earth,
Riches in glory—since thou hast made known
Thy goodness to me on my journeying !"
He sat him by the Guardian of the sea,
That noble saint beside his noble Lord.
I never heard men tell of comelier ship   360
Laden with sumptuous treasures. In it sat
Great heroes, glorious lords, and beauteous thanes.
Then spake the ever-living noble Lord,
Almighty King ; he bade his angel go,
His glorious retainer, go and give

Meat to the desolate to comfort him
Upon the seething flood, that he might bear
The life upon the rushing of the waves
With greater ease.   Then was the ocean[1] stirred
And deeply troubled, then the horn-fish played,   370
Shot through the raging deep ; the sea-gull gray,
Greedy for slaughter, flew in circling flight.
The candle of the sky grew straightway dark,
The winds waxed strong, the waves whirled, and the surge
Leapt high, the ropes creaked, dripping with the waves ;
The Terror of the waters rose, and stood
Above them with the might of multitudes.
The thanes were sore afraid, not one of them
Dared hope that he would ever reach the land,
Of those who by the sea had sought a ship
With Andrew, for as yet they did not know   380
Who pointed out the course for that sea-bark.

When he had eaten, then the faithful thane,
Saint Andrew, thanked the noble Counselor,
Upon the ocean, on the oar-swept sea :—
" For this repast may God, the righteous Lord,
Ruler of hosts, who sheds the light of life,
Grant thee reward, and give thee for thy food
The bread of heaven, e'en as thou hast shown
Good will and kindness to me on the deep.   390
My thanes, these warriors young, are sore afraid ;
Loud roars the raging, overwhelming sea ;
The ocean is all troubled, deeply moved ;
And weary is my band, my company
Of valiant-hearted men, afflicted sore."
The Lord of men gave answer from the helm :—

[1] Lit. " whale-sea."

" Our ship shall bear us back across the flood
Unto the land, and there thy men can wait
Upon the shore until thou come again."   400
Straightway those men gave answer unto him,
Thanes much-enduring ; they would not consent
To leave alone upon the vessel's prow
Their master dear, and choose themselves the land.
" O whither shall we turn us, lordless men,
Mourning in heart, forsaken quite by God,
Wounded with sin, if we abandon thee?
We shall be odious in every land,
Hated of every folk, when sons of men,
Courageous warriors, in council sit   410
And question which of them did best stand by
His lord in battle, when the hand and shield,
Worn out by broadswords on the battle-plain,
Suffered sore danger in the sport of war."

Then spake the noble Lord, the faithful King ;
Straightway He lifted up His voice and said :—
" If, as thou sayst, thou art indeed a thane
Of Him who sits enthroned in majesty,
All-glorious King, expound His mysteries,
How 'neath the sky He taught speech-uttering men. 420
Long is this journey o'er the fallow flood ;
Comfort the hearts of thy disciples ; great
Is yet our way across the ocean-stream,
And land is far to seek ; the sea is stirred,
The waves beat on the shore.   Yet easily
Can God give aid to men who sail the deep."

Then Andrew wisely stablished by his words
His followers, those heroes glorious :—

14

" Ye did consider when ye put to sea
That ye would bear your life unto a folk   430
Of foemen ; ye would suffer death for love
Of God, would give your life within the realm
Of dark-skinned Ethiopians.   I know
Myself that there is One who shieldeth us,
The Maker of the angels, Lord of hosts.
Rebuked and bridled by the King of might,
The Terror of the waters shall grow calm,
The leaping sea.   So once in days of yore
Within a bark upon the struggling waves
We tried the waters, riding on the surge,
And very fearful seemed the sad sea-roads.   440
The ocean-floods beat fierce against the shores ;
Oft wave would answer wave ; and whiles upstood
From out the ocean's bosom, o'er our ship,
A Terror on the breast of our sea-boat.
There on that ocean-courser bode His time
The glorious God, Creator of mankind,
Almighty One.   The men were filled with fear,
They sought protection, mercy from the Lord.
And when that company began to call,
The King straightway arose, and stilled the waves,   450
The seething of the waters—He who gives
Bliss to the angels ; He rebuked the winds ;
The sea subsided, and the boundaries
Of ocean-stream grew calm.   Then laughed our soul,
When under heaven's course our eyes beheld
The winds and waves and Terror of the deep
Affrighted by the Terror of the Lord.
Therefore I say to you in very sooth,
The ever-living God does not forsake
A man on earth, if courage fail him not."   460

15

Thus spake the holy champion, wise of heart,
He taught his thanes, that blessed warrior;
He stablishèd his men, till suddenly
Sleep came upon them weary by the mast.
The sea grew still, the onset of the waves
Turned back again, rough tumult of the flood.
Then was the soul of that brave saint rejoiced,
After that time of terror; wise in wit,
In counsel prudent, he began to speak
And thus unlocked the treasure of his words:—   470
"I never found a better mariner,
More skilled than thou in sea-craft, as I think,
A stouter oarsman, one more wise in words,
Sager in counsel. I will beg of thee
Yet one more boon, hero most excellent;
Though little treasure I can give to thee,
Jewels or beaten gold, I fain would win
Thy friendship, if I might, most glorious lord.
So shalt thou gain good gifts, and blessed joy   480
In heavenly glory, if of thy great lore
Thou'rt bountiful to weary voyagers.
One art I fain would learn of thee, brave sir;
That since the Lord, the Maker of mankind,
Hath given might and honor unto thee,
Thou shouldst instruct me how thou pointest out
The course of this thy billow-riding ship,
Thy sea-horse wet with spray. Though sixteen times,
In former days and late, I've been to sea,   490
And rowed with freezing hands upon the deep,
The ocean-streams—this makes one voyage more—
Yet even so mine eyes have ne'er beheld
A mighty captain steering at the stern
Like unto thee. Loud roars the surging flood,

16

Beats on the shore; this sea-boat is full fleet;
It fareth foamy-necked most like a bird,
And glides upon the deep.   I surely know,
I never saw upon the ocean-road
Such wondrous skill in any seafarer.   500
It is as though the ship were on the land,
Where neither storm nor wind can make it move,
Nor water-floods can break it, lofty-prowed ;
Yet on the sea it hasteth under sail.
And thou art young, defense of warriors,
Not old in winters, rider of the surge ;
Yet in thy heart thou hast the noble speech
Of princes, and dost wisely understand
All words employed by men upon the earth."

Him answered then the everlasting Lord :—   510
"Full oft it happens when we sail the sea
That with our ships, our ocean-coursing steeds,
We break our way across the watery roads ¹—
We and our seamen—when the tempest comes,
And many times we suffer sore distress
Upon the waves, though sailing bravely on
We end our journey ; for the seething flood
Can hinder no man 'gainst the Maker's will.
The power of life He holds—He who doth bind
The billows, and doth threaten and rebuke
The dusky waves.   With justice He shall rule   520
The nations—He who raised the firmament,
And made it fast with His own hands ; who wrought
And did uphold ; and with His glory filled
Bright Paradise—so was the angels' home
Made blessèd by His sole eternal might.

¹ Lit. "bath-road."

The truth is manifest and clear to all,
That thou art thane most excellent of Him,
The King who sits enthroned in majesty ;
Because the swelling ocean knew thee straight,
The circuit of the raging ocean knew
That thou didst have the Holy Spirit's gifts.   530
The sea, the mingling waves, turned back again ;
Still grew the Terror, the wide-bosomed flood ;
The waves subsided straightway when they saw
That God had girt thee with His covenant,
He who did stablish by His own strong might
The blessedness of glory without end."

   Then spake with holy voice the champion
Valiant of heart ; he magnified the King
Who rules in glory, speaking thus in words :—
"Blest art Thou, King of men, Redeeming Lord ;   540
Thy power endureth ever ; near and far
Thy name is holy, bright with majesty,
Renowned in mercy 'mong the tribes of men.
There lives no man beneath the vault of heaven,
Ruler of nations, Savior of men's souls,
No one of mortal race, who can declare
How gloriously Thou dealest Thy good gifts,
Or tell their number.   It is manifest
That Thou has been most gracious to this youth,   550
And hast adorned him with Thy holy grace,
Young as he is ; for he is wise in wit
And in discourse of words.   I never found
A mind more prudent in a man so young."

   The Glory of kings, the Source and End of all,
Gave answer from the ship and boldly asked :—

"Tell, if thou canst, O prudent-minded thane,
How on the earth it ever came to pass
That faithless men, the nation of the Jews,
Raised blasphemy against the Son of God   560
With hearts of wickedness. Unhappy men,
Cruel, malicious, they did not believe
In Him who gave them life, that He was God,
Though many miracles among the tribes
He showed full clear and manifest ; but they,
Guilt-laden men, knew not the Royal Child,
Him that was born a comfort and defense
Unto mankind, to all who dwell on earth.
In wisdom and in power of speech increased
The noble Prince ; and aye the Lord of might   570
Showed forth his wonders to that stubborn folk."

   Straightway did Andrew answer him again :—
" How could it happen 'mong the tribes of men
That thou, my friend, hast never heard men tell
The Savior's power, how He made known His grace
Throughout the world—Son of the Mighty One.
Speech gave He to the dumb ; the deaf did hear ;
The halt and lepers He made glad in heart,
Those who long time had suffered, sick of limb,
Weary and weak, fast bound in misery.   580
Throughout the towns the blind received their sight,
Full many men upon the plains of earth
He woke from death by His almighty word ;
And many another miracle He showed,
Royally famous, by His mighty strength.
Water He blessed before the multitude,
And bade it turn to wine, a better kind,
For happiness of men. Likewise He fed

Five thousand of mankind with fishes twain   590
And with five loaves ; the companies sat down
With hearts fatigued, rejoicing in their rest,
All weary after wandering ; on the ground
Where pleased them best the men received their food.
Lo, thou mayst hear, good sir, how, while He lived,
The Lord of glory by His words and deeds
Showed love to us-ward, led us by His lore
To that fair home of joy where men may dwell
Freely with angels in high blessedness—
Even they who after death go to the Lord."   600

Again the Ruler of the waves unlocked
The treasure of His words, and boldly spake :—
"That I may truly know, I pray thee tell
Whether thy Lord showed forth His miracles—
Which on the earth for comfort of mankind
Full many times He worked—before men's sight,
Where bishops, scribes, and princes held discourse
Sitting in council.   For it seems to me
That out of envy they contrived this guile,   610
Led by deep error and the Devil's lore ;
Those men foredoomed to death too readily
Gave ear to wicked traitors ; their ill fate
Deceived, misled them, gave them counsel false ;
Weary 'mong weary men they soon must bear
Torments and biting flames in Satan's arms."

Straightway did Andrew answer him again :—
" I tell thee truly that He ofttimes worked
Wonder on wonder in the sight of men,   620
Before their rulers ; and in secret too
The Lord of men did deeds of public good,
Which he devised for their eternal peace."

Him answered then the sure Defense of kings :—
" Couldst thou, wise hero, warrior strong of heart,
Tell me in words the wonders that He showed
In secret, when, as oft, ye sat alone
In converse with the Lord who rules the skies ?"

Straightway did Andrew answer him again —
" Why dost thou question me with crafty speech,
My dearest lord, thou who dost truly know   630
By virtue of thy wisdom every hap."

The Ruler of the waves replied to him :—
" 'Tis not in blame that I thus question thee,
Nor to insult thee on the ocean-road.[1]
My mind is blithe and blossoming with joy
At thy most noble speech ; not I am blithe
Alone, for every man is glad in heart
And comforted in soul who far or near
Remembers in his heart what that One did,
God's Son on earth.   Souls unto Him were turned ; 640
With eagerness they sought the joys of heaven,
The angels' home, by aid of His great might."

Straightway did Andrew answer Him again :—
" In thee I see an understanding heart
Of wondrous power, the gift of victory ;
With wisdom blooms thy breast, with brightest joy.
Lo, I will tell to thee from first to last
The words and wisdom of the noble Lord,   650
As I have heard it oft from His own mouth
When He conversed with men upon the earth.
Oft did great multitudes, unnumbered throngs,

[1] Lit. "whale-road."

21

Assemble to the council of the Lord,
And hear the teachings of the Holy One.
The Shield of kings, bright Giver of all bliss,
Went to another house, where many men,
Wise elders, came to meet Him, praising God ;
And ever men were joyful, glad of heart,
At the Lord's coming.

     Likewise it befell   660
That once of yore the Lord of victory,
The mighty King, went on a pilgrimage ;
Eleven glorious champions alone
Of His own people on that journey went ;
He was Himself the twelfth. When we were come
Unto the kingly city where was built
The temple of the Lord with pinnacles
High towering, famous 'mong the tribes of men,
Beauteous in splendor—with reviling words
The high priest straight began to mock at Him 670
Insultingly, from out his wicked heart ;
He oped his inmost thoughts and mischief wove ;
For in his heart he knew we followed aye
The footsteps of our ever-righteous Lord,
His teachings we performed ; straightway he raised
His baneful voice infect with wickedness :—
' Lo, ye are wretched more than all mankind ;
Ye go upon wide wanderings, and ye fare
On many toilsome journeys ; ye give ear
Unto a stranger's teachings 'gainst our law ;
A prince without a portion ye proclaim ;   680
Ye say, in sooth, that with the Son of God
Ye daily converse hold ! The rulers know
From what beginning his high race is sprung.

In this land he was nourished, and was born
A child among his kindred ; at their home
Thus are his father and his mother called—
As we have learned by prudent questioning—
Mary and Joseph ; other children twain
Were born his brothers in that family, 690
Simon and Jacob—Joseph's sons they are.'
So spake the counsellors of men, the lords
Ambitious, and they thought to hide the might
Of God ; their sin returned to them again
From whom it rose, an everlasting bane.

Then did the Prince, the Lord of hosts, depart
With all His thanes from out the council-hall,
Strong in His might, to seek an unknown land.
By wonders manifold and mighty deeds
In deserts wild He showed that He was King 700
By right throughout the world, made strong with power,
Ruler and Author of bright majesty,
Eternal God of all created things.
Likewise He showed before the sight of men
Unnumbered other works miraculous.

Upon another journey then He went
With a vast throng, and in the temple stood,
The glorious Prince. The sound of words arose
Within the lofty building ; sinful men
Would not receive the holy Savior's words,
Though He had shown so many tokens true 710
While they looked on. Upon the temple wall
On either side the Lord victorious saw
An image of His angels wondrous carved,
Brightly adorned and beautifully wrought ;

Then to the multitude he spake in words :—
' This is the likeness of the angel-race
Most widely known to dwellers in this town.
In Paradise their names are Cherubim   720
And Seraphim ; before the face of God
They stand, strong-souled, and with their voices praise
In holy song the might of Heaven's King,
And God's protecting hand.   Here is carved out
The holy angels' form ; the thanes of glory
Are chiseled on the wall by handicraft.'

The Lord of hosts, the Holy Spirit of heaven,
Spake yet again unto the multitude :—
' Now I command a sign to be disclosed,
A miracle before the throng of men,   730
That from the wall this image shall descend
All beautiful to earth, and speak a word,
Shall tell them truly of My parentage,
That men throughout the land may then believe ! '

The ancient image durst not disobey
The Savior's words, but leapt from off the wall,
Stone cleft from stone ; upon the earth it stood,
A wonder in the sight of all the throng ;
Then came a voice loud sounding from the stone,   740
Rebuking them in words ; and wondrous seemed
The statue's speech to those proud-hearted men.
With tokens manifest it taught the priests,
Warned them with wisdom ; thus it spake in words :—
'Accursed are ye and wretched in your thoughts,
Deceived with tricks, or else with clouded mind
No better do ye know.   Ye call God's Son
Eternal but a man—Him who marked out

With His own hands the sea and solid ground,
Both heaven and earth, the stormy ocean-waves,
The salt sea-streams, and the high firmament.   750
He is that self-same God all-powerful
Whom in the early days your fathers knew ;
To Abraham, to Isaac, and to Jacob
He gave His grace, and honored them with wealth ;
To Abraham He first declared in words
The covenant of his race, that of his seed
The God of glory should be born ; this fate
Is now fulfilled among you, manifest ;
And lo ! your eyes can now behold the God
Of victory, who rules the heavens on high.'   760

   After these words the crowd stood listening ;
All silent were they through the spacious hall.
The elders then began again to say,
Those sinful men—the truth they did not know !—
That it was magic art and sorcery
That made the shining stone to talk to men.
Evil was blossoming in their hearts, and hate
Welled hot as fire within their wicked breasts,
A serpent, foe to joy, a poison dire ;   770
And by their words of mocking were revealed
Their doubting hearts and thoughts of wickedness,
With murder girt about.   Then did the Lord
Command the stone, that mighty work, to go
Along the way, from out the open place,
To tread the paths of earth, the meadows green,
To bear God's message into Canaan land,
And in God's name command that Abraham
And his descendants twain should rise again

From out their sepulchre, and leave their place   780
Of rest beneath the earth, take up their limbs,
Receive a soul again and youth's estate ;
That those wise patriarchs should come once more
Among mankind, to tell the folk what God
It was that they had known by His own might.

It went and journeyed on the border-paths
As mighty God, Creator of mankind,
Commanded it, until it came to Mamre
All dazzling bright, as God had bidden it.
There had the bodies of those patriarchs   790
Long time lain hid.   It bade them straight arise
From out the earth, those princes, Abraham,
Isaac, and Jacob, leaving their deep sleep
To meet their God ; it bade them to prepare
To come before the presence of the Lord ;
For they must tell the folk Who at the first
Brought forth this earth all-green, and heaven above,
And where that Ruler was who stablished firm
All that great work.   They durst not long delay
Fulfilment of the glorious King's command.   800
So went those prophets three, those valiant men,
And trod the earth ; they let their sepulchres
Stand open, for they would straightway proclaim
The Father of creation.   Then the folk
With fear was stricken, when those Princes old
Honored the King of glory with their words.
The Lord of might bade them forthwith return
To blessedness, to seek a second time
The happiness of heaven in holy peace,
And there to live in bliss for evermore.   810

Lo, thou mayst hear, dear youth, how He performed
By His commands full many miracles ;
Yet even so those people blind of heart
Did not believe His teachings. I could tell
Many more deeds which He, the Prince of heaven,
Wrought on the earth—a great and famous tale :
Such deeds as thou couldst never understand,
Nor comprehend in heart, though thou art wise."
Thus Andrew all day long showed forth the lore
Of holy Jesus in his words, until
A sleep came sudden o'er him as he sailed   820
Upon the whale's road nigh to Heaven's King.

 The Lord of life then bade His angels bear
That saint beloved over the beating waves,
And gently carry him upon their breasts
Under the Father's care across the floods,
While sleep was on him weary of the sea.
So journeying through the air he reached the land
And came unto the city, which the King
Of angels bade him seek ; the messengers
Departed joyful to their home on high.   830
They left the holy man, that gracious saint,
Beside the highway, 'neath the vault of heaven,
Peacefully sleeping near the city wall
And near his foes malignant all night long,
'Till God sent forth the candle of the day
Brightly to shine. Vanished the shadows dark
Beneath the welkin ; then the torch of heaven,
The clear light of the sky, came forth and shone
Above the town. The warrior brave awoke
And gazed upon the fields ; before the gates   840
Steep hills high towered ; about the hoary cliff

Stood buildings wrought of many-colored tiles,
Great towers, and wind-swept walls. The sage straight
   knew
That he had reached the Mermedonian land,
E'en as the Father of mankind declared,
When He prescribed that journey. On the ground
He saw his own disciples, valiant men,
Beside him deep in sleep. He straight began
To wake the warriors ; thus he spake in words :—   850
"Lo, I can tell you one truth manifest,
That yesterday upon the ocean-stream
A noble Hero bore us o'er the sea.
The Glory of kings, the Ruler of mankind,
Was sailing in that ship ; I knew His words,
Though He did hide the beauty of His face."

His noble followers answered him again,
Giving reply from out their inmost souls :—
" Our journey, Andrew, will we tell to thee,
That wisely thou mayst understand in heart :—   860
A sleep came o'er us weary of the sea,
And eagles came across the struggling waves
In flight, exulting in their mighty wings,
And while we slept they took our souls away ;
With joy they bore us flying through the air,
Gracious and bright, rejoicing in their speed;
And gently they caressed us, while they hymned
Continual praise ; there was unceasing song
Throughout the sky; a beauteous host was there,   870
A glorious multitude. The angels stood
About the Prince, the thanes about their Lord,
In thousands; in the highest they gave praise
With holy voice unto the Lord of lords ;

The angel-band rejoiced. We there beheld
The holy patriarchs and a mighty troop
Of martyrs ; to the Lord victorious
That righteous throng sang never-ending praise ;
And David too was with them, Jesse's son,
The King of Israel, blessed warrior,   880
Come to Christ's throne. Likewise we saw you twelve
All standing there before the Son of God,
Full glorious men of great nobility ;
Archangels holy throned in majesty
Did serve you ; happy is it for the man
Who may enjoy that bliss. High joy was there,
Glory of warriors, an exalted life ;
Nor was there sorrow there for any man.
Drear exile, open torment is the lot
Of him who must be stranger to those joys,   890
And wander wretched when he goes from hence."

   Exceeding glad was holy Andrew's heart
Within his breast, soon as he heard the speech
Of his disciples, that above all men
God should so high esteem them, and this word
Spake then the brave defense of warriors :—
" Lo, now I clearly see, Lord God, that Thou,
Glory of kings, wast very nigh to me
On the ocean-road, when on that ship I went ;
Though on the beating sea I did not know   900
The Lord of angels, Savior of men's souls !
Be gracious unto me, Almighty God,
Bright King of mercy ! on the ocean-stream
Full many words I spake ; but now I know
Who bore me o'er the sea-floods on His ship
With honor high ; He is for all mankind

A Spirit of comfort ; there is ready help,
And mercy from the Highest unto all
Who seek of Him—the gift of victory."

Straightway before his eyes the Lord appeared,   910
The Prince of glory, King of all that lives,
Like to a youth in form, and thus he spake :—
" Hail to thee, Andrew, and thy faithful band ;
Rejoice in heart, for I am thy defense,
That wicked foes may never harm thy soul,
Fierce-hearted workers of iniquity."

Then fell to earth that hero wise in words,
Begging protection, and he asked his Lord :—
" How did it happen, Ruler of mankind,   920
That, sinning 'gainst the Savior of men's souls,
I knew Thee not upon the ocean-way
Good as Thou art ? there spake I many words,
More than I should in presence of my God."

Him answered straightway God all-powerful :—
" Thou didst not sin so grievously as when
Thou madest protest in Achaian land
That on far journeyings thou couldst not go,
Nor come unto the town, accomplishing
Thy way within three days, the time ordained,   930
As o'er the struggling waves I bade thee fare.
Thou knowest better now that easily
I can advance and further any man
Who is My friend whithersoe'er I will.
Quickly arise, and straightway learn My will,
Man highly blessed ; so shall the Father bright
Adorn thee with His wondrous gifts, with strength

And wisdom unto all eternity !
Go thou into the town, within the walls,
Where bides thy brother ; for I know full well   940
Matthew thy kinsman is afflicted sore
With deadly wounds at wicked traitors' hands,
Beset with cunning snares. Him shalt thou seek
And loose from hate of foes, with all that band
Who dwell with him in strangers' cruel chains
Balefully bound. Forthwith he shall receive
In this world recompense, and high reward
In heaven, as I have promised unto him.
Now, Andrew, thou shalt straightway risk thy life   950
Into the foeman's grasp ; for thee is war
Ordained with grievous sword-blows ; with sore wounds
Thy body shall be rent ; thy blood shall flow
In floods like water. But those foes may not
Give o'er thy life to death, though heavy strokes,
The blows of sinful men, thou undergo.
Endure that grief ; let not the heathens' might
Turn thee aside, nor bitter strife of spears,
That thou depart from God who is thy Lord.
Be eager aye for glory, bear in mind   960
How it was widely known to many men,
Through many lands, that sinners mocked at Me
Bound fast in chains, reviled Me with their words,
Struck Me and scourged Me ; with their taunting speech
Those sinful men could not declare the truth.
When 'mong the Jews I hung upon the cross,
When high the rood was raised, a certain man
Let forth the blood from out My wounded side
Upon the ground. Full many grievous woes
I suffered on the earth; I wished to give   970
A high example to you by My grace,

Which shall be known 'mong men of foreign land.
Many there are within this famous town
Whom thou shalt turn unto the light of heaven
In My name, though they have in days gone by
Accomplished many deeds of violence."
The Holy One departed, King of kings,
In blessedness to seek the heavens above,
That purest home; there is for every man
Glory enow, for those who can attain.   980

 That much-enduring man, brave for the fight,
Obeyed God's word; he went into the town
Forthwith, that steadfast warrior, with might
Endowed, courageous-hearted, true to God;
He walked along the street, the path his guide,
In such wise that no one could him behold,
No sinful man could see, for on the mead
The Lord victorious had covered him,
That chief beloved, with His protecting care
And His high favor. So the noble saint   990
Nigh to the prison pressed his way in haste,
The champion of Christ. He saw a band
Of heathens gathered, seven warders there
Before the gate; death snatched them all away;
They perished powerless; the fierce rush of death
Clutched them all bloody. Then the holy saint
Prayed to the gracious Father in his heart;
He praised on high the goodness and the power
Of Heaven's King. The door forthwith gave way
At holy Andrew's touch; then entered in   1000
The hero brave with thoughts of courage bold.
The heathens there were sleeping drunk with blood;
With their own blood they stained the field of death.

The Legend of St. Andrew

Matthew he saw within that murderous den,
The warrior stout, within the prison mirk,
Singing the praise of God, and worshiping
The angels' King. Alone he sat in grief
In that drear dwelling. On this earth once more
His brother dear he saw—a holy saint
Beheld a holy saint—and hope grew strong.   1010
Up rose he quick to meet him, thanking God
That 'neath the sun they had at last beheld
Each other hale and sound. New joy and love
Dwelt with those brethren twain ; each in his arms
Enclosed the other ; they embraced and kissed.
Unto the heart of Christ both saints were dear.
A holy radiance bright as heaven above
Shone round about them, and their hearts welled up
With joy. Then first did Andrew greet in words   1020
His noble comrade, that God-fearing man :
He told him of the battle that must come,
The fight of hostile men :—   .   .   .

      .   .   .   .

      .   .   .   .

After these words those brothers knelt and prayed,
Those thanes of glory, and they sent their prayer
Up to the Son of God ; and Matthew too
Within the prison called upon his God,   1030
Sought from the Savior succor and relief
Before he should be slain by battle-might
Of heathen men. Then from the prison strong,
Freed from their bonds, protected by the Lord,
He led two hundred men and forty-eight
Rescued from woe ; not one he left behind
Within the prison-walls fast bound in chains ;

And women too, besides this multitude,
Fifty less one he saved, o'erwhelmed with fear.   1040
Glad were they to depart, in haste they went,
Nor waited longer in that house of woe
The outcome of the struggle. ' Matthew went
Leading that multitude, as Andrew bade,
Under God's keeping ; on that longed-for way
He covered them with clouds, lest enemies,
Their ancient foes, should come to work them harm
With arrows' flight ; there did those valiant saints
Take counsel with each other, faithful friends,
Before they parted ; each of those brave men   1050
Stablished the other with the hope of heaven ;
The pains of hell they warded off by words.
So did the warriors with them, battle-brave,
Tried champions, with their holy voices praise
The Lord of fate, whose glory ne'er shall end.

Glad-hearted, Andrew walked about the town
Unto the place where he had heard was met
A concourse of his cruel enemies,   1060
Until he found beside the border-path
A brazen pillar standing near the road.
He sat him by its side ; pure love had he
And contemplation high, the angels' bliss ;
There waited he, within the city-walls,
What deed of war should be vouchsafed to him.

Then gathered straight the leaders of the folk
Their mighty troops ; unto the prison strong
The faithless host of heathen warriors
Came fully armed, where late their captive thralls   1070
Had suffered woe within the prison mirk.

They weened and wished, those stubborn-hearted foes,
That they might make those foreign men their meat,
Food for the multitude ; their hope was vain,
For, coming with their troops, those spearmen fierce
Found prison-doors wide open, and the work
Of hammers all unloosed, the watchmen dead.
So back they turned, those luckless warriors,
Robbed of their joy, to bear the tidings sad ;
They told the folk that of the stranger men,   1080
The men of foreign speech, not one they found
Remaining in that prison-house alive ;
But there upon the ground all stained with gore,
Lifeless the watchmen lay, robbed of their souls,
Mere slaughtered bodies. At that sudden news
Dismayed was many a captain of the host,
Sad and cast down at thoughts of famine stern,
That pale guest at the board. No better way
They knew than on the dead to make their feast
For their own sustenance ; in a single hour   1090
The bed of death was spread by cruel fate
For all those watchmen.

Then, as I have heard,
A gathering of the townsmen was proclaimed ;
The heroes came, a host of warriors
Riding on horses, brave men on their steeds
Exchanging speech ; skilled were they at the spear.
So in the meeting-place the people all
Were gathered, and they bade the lot decide
Among them, who should first give up his life   1100
For food unto the rest ; they cast the lots
With hellish craft ; before their heathen gods
They counted them. Behold, the lot did fall

35

Upon an aged chieftain, one who was
A counselor among the noble lords,
In front rank of the host.   Soon was he bound
In fetters fast, despairing of his life.

Then cried that chieftain fierce with voice of woe,
Proclaiming he would give his own young son
Into their power as ransom for his life.   1110
With thankful hearts they took his offering,
For greedily they lusted after food,
Sad-minded men ; no joy had they in wealth,
Nor hope in hoarded riches ; they were sore
Oppressed with hunger, for the famine dire
Held cruel sway.   Then many a warrior
And hero battle-bold was fired in heart
To struggle for the life of that young man ;
The sign of woe was published far and wide
Throughout the town to many a hero brave,   1120
That they should seek in troops the young man's death,
That, young and old, they should receive their share
As food to keep their lives.   The heathen priests
Straightway collected there a multitude
Of dwellers in that town ; loud shouts arose.

Bound there before the throng the youth began
To sing with mournful voice a song of woe ;
The wretched thrall begged succor of his friends ;
But no relief nor mercy could he find
From that fierce folk to give him back his life.   1130
Those monstrous fiends had sought hostility ;
It was their purpose that the sword's sharp edge
Made hard by blows, and stained with marks of fire,

In foeman's hand should take his life away.
But Andrew thought it grievous, hard to bear,
A public wrong, that one so innocent
Should forthwith lose his life. That people's hate
Was very fierce ; the warriors, valiant thanes   1140
Lusting for murder, rushed upon the youth ;
They wished straightway to break his head with spears.
But God, the Holy One, from heaven above
Defended him against the heathen throng ;
He bade their weapons melt away like wax
In the fierce onset, that his bitter foes
Should scathe him not with might of hostile swords.
So from his woe and from that people's hate
The youth was loosed. To God, the Lord of lords,   1150
Be thanks for all, because He giveth might
To every man who wisely seeketh aid
From Him on high ! There is eternal peace
Ever prepared for those who can attain.   ·

Then in that town was lamentation heard,
Loud outcry of the throng ; heralds proclaimed
And mourned the lack of food ; there stood they sad,
Held fast by hunger ; the high-towering halls—
Their wine-halls—all were empty ; they possessed
No wealth to enjoy at that unhappy hour.   1160
The wise men sat apart in council sad,
Talked of their woe ; no joy was in their land.
Thus would one hero oft another ask :—
" Let him who has good counsel in his heart,
And wisdom, hide it not ! The hour is come
Exceeding woful ; great is now the need
That we should hear the words of prudent men."

Then to that band the Devil straight appeared
All black and ugly, and he had the form
Of one accursed. The Prince of death began,   1170
The limping imp of hell, with wicked heart
To accuse the holy man; this word he spake :—
"A certain prince is come into your town,
A stranger journeying from a distant land ;
Andrew I heard him called. He worked you scath
But lately, when he led a company
Great beyond measure from your prison strong ;
And now these deeds of harm ye may with ease
Wreak on their author ; let your weapons' point,   1180
Your hard-edged iron, hew his body down,
Doomed to destruction. Go now boldly forth,
That ye may overcome your foe in war."

Straightway did Andrew answer him again :—
"Why dost thou impudently teach this folk,
And urge them unto battle ? Hast thou felt
The fiery torment hot in hell, and yet
Leadest an army forth, a troop to war ?
Thou art a foe to God, the Lord of hosts ;
Why dost thou thus heap up thy wretchedness ?
Shaft of the devil, whom Almighty God   1190
Bent humble down and into darkness hurled,
Where the King of kings did cover thee with chains ;
And they who keep the covenant of God
Have called thee Satan ever since that hour."

Again the Adversary by his words,
With fiendish craft urged on the folk to fight :—
" Now do you hear the foeman of your tribe,
Him who has wrought most harm unto this host !

Andrew it is, who thus disputes with me
In cunning words before the throng of men."   1200
Then to the townsmen was the signal given;
Up leaped they valiant with the shout of hosts,
And to the city-gates the warriors thronged
Bold 'neath their banners; with their spears and shields,
In mighty troops they pressed unto the fight.

  Then spake the Lord of hosts, Almighty God,
And said these words unto His valiant thane :—
"O Andrew, thou shalt do a deed of might ;
Shrink not before this host, but thy brave heart
Strengthen against the strong! The hour is nigh   1210
When these blood-thirsty men shall weigh thee down
With torments and cold chains. Reveal thyself,
Make firm thy soul, and strengthen thy brave heart,
That they may recognize My power in thee!
They cannot and they may not, crime-stained men,
Deal death unto thy body 'gainst My will,
Though thou shalt suffer many evil blows
From murderers. Lo, I abide with thee! "

  After these words there came a countless throng,
False leaders with their troops of shield-clad men,   1220
Angry at heart. Straight rushed they out and bound
Saint Andrew's hands, soon as the joy of lords
Revealed himself, and they could see him there
Boldly triumphant. Many a warrior
Lusted for battle on that field of death,
Among the host of men. Little they cared
What recompense hereafter they should find.
They gave command to lead their hated foe
Over the country, and from time to time   1230

To drag him fiercely as they could contrive.
Savage, they haled him, cruel-hearted foes,
Through mountain-caves, about the stony cliffs,
Far as their stone-paved streets and highways stretched—
The ancient work of giants—through the town.
A tumult and a mighty outcry rose
Within the city from the heathen host.
With grievous wounds was Andrew's body pained,
Broken and wet with blood, which welled in streams 1240
All hot with gore ; yet had he in his breast
Courage undoubting ; and his noble mind
Was free from sin, though he was doomed to bear
Such bitter suffering from his heavy wounds.

Thus all day long till radiant evening came
Was Andrew scourged ; and yet a second day
Pain pierced his breast, until the gleaming sun
With heavenly radiance to his setting went.
Then to the prison did those people lead
Their hated foe ; yet to the heart of Christ   1250
Was he full dear ; within his holy breast
His soul shone bright—a mind invincible.
So all night long the hero brave of heart,
That holy saint, dwelt 'neath the gloomy shades,
Beset with cunning snares. Snow bound the earth
In wintry storms ; the air grew bitter cold
With heavy showers of hail ; the rime and frost,
Those warriors hoary, locked the homes of men,
The people's dwellings ; frozen were the lands
With icicles ; the water's might shrank up   1260
Within the rivers, and the ice bridged o'er
The gleaming water-roads. The noble saint
Abode blithe-hearted, planning valiant deeds,

Bold and courageous in his misery,
Throughout the wintry night ; nor did he e'er,
Dismayed by terror, cease to praise the Lord,
And ever worship Him, as at the first,
With righteous heart, until the radiant gem
Of glory rose.

Then came a mighty troop,
A throng of warriors thirsting after blood,   1270
With clamor loud unto the prison mirk.
They gave command to lead the noble saint,
That steadfast man, into his foemen's grasp ;
And once again he suffered all day long,
Beaten with grievous blows ; his blood welled out
In streams o'er all his body. .   .   .   .
. . . . . . Worn with wounds
He scarce felt any pain. Then from his breast
The sound of weeping issued faintly forth,
A stream welled up, and thus he spake in words :— 1280
"O God, my Lord, behold now mine estate,
Ruler of hosts, Thou who dost understand
And know the misery of every man ;
I trust in Thee, Thou Author of my life,
That, in Thy mercy and Thy glorious power,
O Savior of mankind, Thou never wilt
Forsake me, everlasting God of might ;
So while my life shall last I ne'er will leave,
O God, Thy gracious teachings ! Lo, Thou art   1290
A shield against the weapons of the foe
For all Thy saints, eternal Source of joy.
Let not man's foe, the first-born child of sin,
Revile me now, nor by his fiendish craft
Cover with woe the men who spread Thy praise."

Then in their midst the ugly fiend appeared,
That wicked traitor damned to torments sharp ;
Before the host he taught the warriors,
The Devil of hell, and this word did he speak :—
"Come, smite the wicked wretch upon his mouth, 1300
The foeman of this folk ; too much he talks !"

Then was the strife stirred up once more anew,
And violence arose, until the sun
Went to his setting 'neath the gloomy earth;
Night shrouded all, and spread o'er mountains steep,
A dusky brown. Then to the prison mirk
Once more the brave and righteous saint was led,
And all night long that true man had to dwell
Within his wretched den, the house unclean. 1310

Then came unto the hall with other six
That demon vile, mindful of evil deeds,
The lord of murder, shrouded in deep gloom,
The Devil fierce, bereft of majesty,
And to the saint he spake reviling words :—
"Andrew, why didst thou plan thy coming here,
Into the power of foes? Where is that fame
Which in thy arrogance thou didst set up,
When thou wouldst overthrow our gods' renown ?
Thou hast claimed all things for thyself alone, 1320
The land and people, as thy master did ;
He set up royal power upon the earth,
As long as it might stand—Christ was his name.
Herod, the king, deprived him of his life,
He overcame the King of the Jews in war,
Robbed him of power, and nailed him on the rood,
That on the cross he might give up his life.

So now I bid my sons, my mighty thanes,
To vanquish thee, his follower, in the fight.
Let javelin-point and arrow poison-dipped   1330
Pierce his doomed breast !   Advance, ye bold of heart,
That ye may humble low this warrior's pride !"

    Fierce-souled were they, and quickly rushed they on
With greedy hands ; but God defended him,
Guiding him steadfast by His own strong might.
Soon as they recognized upon his face
The glorious token of Christ's holy cross,
They all were terrified in the attack,
Sorely afraid, thrown headlong into flight.   1340

    The ancient fiend, the prisoner of hell,
Began once more to sing his mournful song :—
" What happened, O my warriors so bold,
My shield-companions, that ye fared so ill ? "

    An ill-starred wretch, a fiend of wicked heart,
Gave answer then, and to his father said :—
" We shall not quickly work him any harm,
Nor slay him by our wiles ; go thou to him ;
There wilt thou surely find a bitter fight,
A savage battle, if again thou dar'st   1350
To risk thy life against that lonely man.
Much better counsel in the play of swords
We easily can give thee, lord beloved :
Before thou shalt resort to open war
And battle-rush, see to it how thou fare
In that exchange of blows ; but let us go
Again, that we may mock him fast in bonds,
And taunt him with his misery ; have words
Ready devised against that wicked wretch."

Then with a mighty voice cried out that fiend   1360
Weighed down with torments, and this word he spake:—
"Long time, O Andrew, hast thou been well versed
In arts of sorcery ; thou hast deceived
And led astray much people ; but thou shalt
No longer now have power upon such works,
For grievous torments are decreed for thee
According to thy deeds. With weary heart,
Joyless, degraded, thou shalt suffer woes,
The bitter pangs of death. My warriors
Are ready for the battle ; they will soon
Deprive thee of thy life by valiant deeds.   1370
What man on earth so mighty that he may
Release thee from thy bonds, if I oppose?"

Straightway did Andrew answer him again :—
"Almighty God with ease can rescue me
From all my grief—He who in days of yore
Fettered thee fast with fiery chains in woe.
There, shorn of glory, bound with torments fierce,
In exile hast thou dwelt e'er since the day   1380
When thou didst set at naught the word of God,
Of Heaven's King ; then did thy woe begin,
And to thy exile there shall be no end ;
But thou shalt still heap up thy wretchedness
To everlasting life, and evermore
Thy lot shall grow yet harsher day by day."
Then fled that fiend who in the years long past
Began a deadly feud against his God.

Then at the dawning, when the day first broke,
A troop of heathens came to find the saint,
A mighty throng, and gave command to lead   1390

44

That valiant-hearted thane a third time forth.
They wished straightway to overcome the soul
Of that bold saint—but it was not to be.
Then was the battle stirred up once again,
Cruel and very fierce. The holy man,
Bound fast with cunning skill, was sorely scourged,
Pierced through with wounds, until the daylight failed ;
And, sad of heart, he cried aloud to God
Bravely from prison with his holy voice ;
Weary of soul, he spake these words with tears :— 1400
" Ne'er have I suffered by God's holy will
A lot more grievous under heaven's vault,
In lands where I have had to preach His law !
My limbs are wrenched apart, my body sore
Is broken, and my flesh is stained with blood ;
My thews are torn and bloody. Lo, Thou too,
Ruler of victory, Redeeming Lord,
Wast filled with grief among the Jews that day
When from the cross, Thou, everlasting God,
Glory of kings, creation's mighty Lord,   1410
Called to the Father, and thus spake to him :—
'Father of angels, source of light and life,
Oh why hast Thou forsaken me, I pray ?'
Torments most cruel I have had to bear
For three long days. I beg thee, Lord of hosts,
That I may give my soul into Thy hands,
Thy very hands, Thou Nourisher of souls !
For Thou didst promise by Thy holy word,
When Thou didst stablish us, the chosen Twelve,
That we should ne'er be scathed by foeman's sword, 1420
No member of our bodies be destroyed,
No bone nor sinew left beside the way ;
That no lock should be lost from off our heads,

If we would keep Thy teachings faithfully.
My sinews now are loosed, my blood is spilled ;
My hair lies scattered wide upon the ground,
And death were dearer far than this sad life."

Then spake a voice unto that steadfast man ;
The King of glory's words resounded clear :—   1430
"Weep not, O man beloved, at this thy woe ;
Too hard it is not for thee ; with My aid,
With My protection, I will hold thee up,
And compass thee about with My great might.
All power is given to Me upon this earth,
And glorious victory.   Full many a man
Shall bear Me witness at the judgment day,
That all this beauteous world, the heavens and earth,
Shall fall in ruin, before a single word
Which I have spoken with My mouth shall fail.   1440
Look now where thou hast walked, and where thy blood
Was spilled, where from thy wounds the path was stained
With spots of blood.   No more harsh injury
Can they do unto thee by stroke of spears
Who most have harmed thee by their cruel deeds."
Then looked behind him that dear champion,
Even as the glorious King commanded him ;
Fair flowering trees beheld he standing there,
With blossoms decked, where he had shed his blood.

Then spake in words that shield of warriors :—   1450
"Ruler of nations, thanks and praise to Thee
And glory in heaven both now and evermore,
For that Thou didst not leave me in my woe,
Alone, a stranger, Lord of victory ! "
So to the Lord that doer of great deeds

Gave praise with holy voice until the sun
In glorious brightness went beneath the waves.

Then yet a fourth time those fierce-hearted foes,
The leaders of the folk, brought back the prince
Unto his prison ; for they hoped to turn   1460
In the dark night the hero's mighty soul.
Then came the Lord unto that prison-house,
Glory of warriors, and with words of cheer
The Guide of life, the Father of mankind,
Greeted His thane and bade him once again
Soundness enjoy :—" From henceforth and for aye
Thou shalt no more bear woe from armèd men."

Freed from the bondage of his grievous pains,   1470
The mighty saint arose and thanked his God.
His beauty was not marred, nor was the hem
Loosed from his cloak, nor lock from off his head ;
No bone was broken, and no bloody wounds
Were in his body, and no injured limb
Wet with his blood through wounding stroke of sword ;
But there he stood by God's most noble might
Whole as before, giving to Him the praise.

Lo, I awhile the story of the saint—
The song of praise of him who did the deeds—
Have set forth here in words, a tale well known,   1480
Beyond my power ; much is there yet to tell—
A weary task—what he in life endured,
From the beginning on ! A wiser man
Upon the earth than I account myself
Must in his heart invent it, one who knows
From the beginning all the misery
Which bravely he endured in cruel wars.

Yet in small parts we further must relate
A portion of that tale.   It has been told
Already how he suffered many woes   1490
From grievous warfare in the heathen town.

   Beside the prison-wall set wondrous fast
He saw great pillars, work of giants old,
All beaten by the storms.   With one of these
He converse held, mighty and bold of heart ;
Prudent and wondrous wise, he spake these words :—
" Give ear, thou marble stone, to God's command,
Before whose presence all created things—
The heavens and earth—stand trembling, when they see
The Father with a countless multitude   [1500
Visit the race of men upon the earth !
Let streams well forth from out thy firm support,
A gushing river; for the King of heaven,
Almighty God, commands thee that straightway
Upon this stubborn-hearted folk thou send
Water wide-flowing for the people's death,
A rushing sea.   Lo, thou art better far
Than gold or treasure ! for the King Himself,
The God of glory, wrote on thee, and showed   1510
His mysteries forth in words ; Almighty God
In ten commandments showed His righteous law,
Gave it to Moses, and true-hearted men
Kept it thereafter, mighty warriors,
Joshua and Tobias, faithful thanes,
God-fearing men.   Now dost thou truly know
That in the days of old the angels' King
Decked thee more fair than all the precious stones.
Now at His holy bidding thou shalt show   1520
If thou hast any knowledge of thy God ! "

Then was there no delay ; straightway the stone
Split open, and a stream came rushing out
And flowed along the ground ; at early dawn
The foaming billows covered up the earth ;
The ocean-flood waxed great ; mead was outpoured
After that day of feasting ! Mail-clad men
Shook off their slumbers ; water deeply stirred
Seized on the earth ; the host was sore dismayed
At terror of the flood ; the youths were doomed,   1530
And perished in the deep ; the rush of war
Snatched them away with tumult of the sea.
That was a grievous trouble, bitter beer ;
The ready cup-bearers did not delay ;
From daybreak on each man had drink to spare.
The might of waters waxed, the men wailed loud,
Old bearers of the spear ; they strove to flee
The fallow stream ; they fain would save their lives
And seek a refuge in the mountain caves,
Firm earth's support. An angel drove them back,   1540
Compassing all the town with gleaming fire,
With savage flames. Wild beat the sea within ;
No troop of men could scape from out the walls.
The waves waxed, and the waters thundered loud ;
The firebrands flew ; the flood welled up in streams.

Then easy was it in that town to find
The song of sorrow sung, and grief bemoaned,
And many a heart afraid, and dirges sad.
The dreadful fire was plain to every eye,   1550
Fierce pillager, the uproar terrible ;
And rushing through the air the blasts of fire
Hurled themselves round the walls ; the floods grew great.
There far and wide was lamentation heard,

The cries of helpless men. Straightway began
One wretched warrior to collect the folk ;
Humble and sad, he spake with mournful voice :—
" Now may ye truly know that we did wrong
When we o'erwhelmed this stranger with our chains,
With bonds of torment, in the prison-house ;   1560
For Fate is crushing us, most fierce and stern—
That is full clear !—And better is it far,
So hold I truth, that we with one accord
Should loose him soon as may be from his bonds,
And beg the holy man to give us help,
Comfort and aid ! Full quickly we shall find
Peace after sorrow, if we seek of him."

    Then Andrew knew the purpose of the folk
Within his heart ; he knew the warriors' might,   1570
The pride of valiant men, was humbled low.
The waters compassed them about, and fierce
The rushing torrent flowed, the flood rejoiced,
Until the welling sea o'ertopped their breasts,
And reached their shoulders. Then the noble saint
Bade the wild flood subside, the storms to cease
About the stony cliffs. Straight walked he out
And left his prison, valiant, firm of soul,
Wise-hearted, dear to God ; for him forthwith
A way was opened through the spreading stream ;   1580
Calm was the field of victory, the earth
Was dry at once where'er he placed his foot.
Blithe-hearted waxed the dwellers in that town,
And glad in soul ; for help was come to pass
After their grief./The flood subsided straight,
And at the saint's behest the storm was stilled,
The waters ceased. Then was the mountain cloven—

The Legend of St. Andrew

A frightful chasm—into itself it drew
The flood, and swallowed up the fallow waves,
The struggling sea—the abyss devoured it all.   1590
Yet not the waves alone it swallowed up ;
But fourteen men, worst caitiffs of the throng,
Went headlong to destruction with the flood
Under the yawning earth.   Then sore afraid
Was many a heart at that calamity ;
They feared the slaughter both of men and wives,
A yet more wretched season of distress,
When once those sin-stained cruel murderers,
Those warriors fierce, plunged headlong down the abyss.
                                                       1600

   Straightway then spake they all with one accord :—
" Now is it plain to see that one true God,
The King of every creature, rules with might—
He who did hither send this messenger
To help the people !   Great is now our need
That we should follow righteousness with zeal."

   Then did the saint give comfort to those men,
He cheered the throng of warriors with his words :—
" Be not too fearful, though the sinful race
Sought ruin, suffered death—the punishment   1610
Due to their sins.   A bright and glorious light
On you is risen if ye but purpose well."
His prayer he sent before the Son of God,
And begged the Holy One to give His aid
Unto those youths who in the ocean-stream
Had lost their life within the flood's embrace,
So that their souls, forsaken by the Lord,
Shorn of their glory, had been borne away
To death and torments in the power of fiends.

51

Saint Andrew's prayer was pleasing unto God,   1620
Almighty One, the Counselor of men ;
He bade the youths, those whom the flood had slain,
Rise up unscathed in body from the ground.
Then straightway stood there up among the throng
Many an ungrown child, as I have heard ;
Body and soul were joined again in one,
Though but a short time gone in flood's fierce rush
They all had lost their lives. Then they received
True baptism and the covenant of peace,   1630
The pledge of glory, God's protecting grace,
Freedom from punishment. The valiant saint,
The craftsman of the King, then bade them build
A church, and make a temple of the Lord
Upon the spot where those young men arose
By baptism, even where the flood sprang forth.
From far and wide the warriors of that town
Gathered in throngs ; both men and women said
That they would faithfully obey his word,
Receive the bath of baptism joyfully   1640
According to God's will, and straightway leave
Their devil-worship and their ancient shrines.
Then noble baptism was exalted high
Among that folk, the righteous law of God
Established 'mong those men—a mighty boon
Unto their country—and the church was blessed.

The messenger of God appointed one,
A man of wisdom tried, of prudent speech,
To be a bishop in that city bright
Over the people, and he hallowed him
By virtue of his apostolic power   1650
Before the multitude for their behoof,—

The Legend of St. Andrew

His name was Platan. Strictly Andrew bade
That they should keep his teachings zealously,
And should work out salvation for their souls.
He told them he was eager to depart,
And fain would leave that city bright with gold,
Their revelry and wealth, their bounteous halls,
And seek a ship beside the breaking sea.
Hard was it for the multitude to bear
That he, their leader, would no longer dwell   1660
Among them there.   But as he journeyed forth
The glorious God straightway appeared to him,
The Lord of hosts, and to His thane He said :—
"[Why dost thou leave this people in such haste ?
For hardly have they turned them from their sin],
This nation from their crimes.   Their minds for death
Are longing, sad of heart they go about,
Their grief bemoaning, men and women both ;
Weeping has come among them, woful hearts,
[Since thou across the floods in thy sea-bark]
Wilt haste away.   Thou shalt not leave this flock
In joy so new, but in My holy Name   1670
Fast stablish thou their hearts!   Within this town,
Abide, O shield of warriors, in their halls
Richly adorned, the space of seven nights,
Then with My favor thou shalt go thy way."

So once again that brave and mighty saint
Returned to seek the Mermedonian town.
In wisdom and in speech the Christians waxed,
After their eyes beheld the glorious thane,
The noble King's apostle.   In the way
Of faith he guided them ; with glory bright
He made them strong ; a countless multitude   1680

53

Of glorious men he led to blessedness,
Toward that most holy home in Heaven's realm,
Where Father, Son, and Holy Comforter
In blessed Trinity hold mighty rule,
World without end, within those mansions fair.
Likewise the saint attacked their idol-shrines,
Banished their devil-worship, and put down
Their errors. Mighty grief and hard to bear
Was that for Satan, when he saw them turn   1690
With hearts of gladness from the halls of hell
At Andrew's teaching to that land more bright,
Where fiends and evil spirits never come.

· Then was the number of the days fulfilled
Which God had set, and had commanded him
That he should linger in that wind-swept town ;
And quickly he made ready for the waves
With joyful heart ; he wished once more to seek
Achaia in his ocean-coursing ship ;   1700
(There was he doomed to lose his life and die
A death of violence. This deed was fraught
With little laughter for his murderer ;
To the jaws of hell he went, and since that day
No solace has that friendless wretch e'er found.)

Then in great companies, as I have heard,
They led unto his ship their master dear,
Men sad of soul ; the heart of many a one
Was welling hot in grief within his breast.
They brought the zealous champion to his ship   1710
Beside the sea-cliffs, and upon the shore
They stood and mourned while they could still behold
The joy of princes sailing o'er the waves,

The path of seals.   They praised the glorious King ;
The throngs cried out aloud, and thus they spake :—
"One and eternal is the God who rules
O'er all created things ; throughout the earth
His might and His dominion far and near
Are magnified.   His glory over all
Shines on His saints in heavenly majesty   1720
Among the angels now and evermore
In splendor fair.   He is a noble King ! "

NOTES

38 f. Lit. "hay and grass oppressed them."

298. Reading āra with Grein.

368. The MS. says hīe (they), with change of subject; for the sake of clearness I have kept Andrew as the subject.

424. Reading sund with Grein.

592. Adopting Siever's reading, rēonigmōde (*Beitr.* X, 506).

656. "another house"; I am at a loss to explain this apparent inconsistency.

713. That there are two images is shown by the Greek.

719. I omit is. The passage as it stands is meaningless.

746. Reading gē mon cīgað, with Cosijn.

826. Lit. "'Till sleep came o'er them weary of the sea"; but Andrew is already asleep. The line is probably corrupt.

828. Something is apparently missing, though the MS. shows no break. Without attempting an emendation I have supplied: "bade him seek," as completing the obvious sense.

1024. At this point a page is missing in the manuscript. It must have corresponded to the end of Chap. 19 and to Chap. 20 of the Greek, in which Andrew and Matthew exchange short speeches, after which Andrew utters a long tirade against the Devil as the author of this woe. I have omitted lines 1023 b, 1024, and 1025, which are meaningless without what has been lost.

1035. The number of men is uncertain. According to the Greek it is 270, but the Homily says 248. The manuscript reads: "two and a hundred by number, also forty," but l. 1036 is evidently deficient. Wülker emends to swylce seofontig. This is unsatisfactory, since the line is metrically deficient, and since, moreover, the regular word for seventy is not seofontig, but hundseofontig. Without venturing an emendation, I have taken the number 248 from the Homily, as being nearer the manuscript than the 270 of the Greek. This similarity is an additional argument for a common Latin original of the poem and the Homily.

1212. The poet has neglected to mention the circumstance, clearly stated in the Greek, that Andrew was still invisible both to the Devil and to the Mermedonians. This makes clear several passages, i. e., ll. 1203, 1212, 1223 f.

1242. Reading untwēonde with Grein and Cosijn.

1276. I have here omitted two half-lines, of which the sense is very obscure. Grein connects lifrum with Germ. *liefern* = " to coagulate " (cf. Eng. *loppered milk*), instead of assigning it to **lifer** = "liver," but this interpretation is not very satisfactory. See also Cosijn's note (Paul und Braune's *Beiträge*, XXI, 17).

1338. The Greek explains that God had put the sign of the cross on Andrew's face.

1376. I have here ventured an emendation of my own. The sentence as it stands is without a main verb, and 1377 [a] is metrically deficient. I would read :—

> Hwæt mē ēaðe [mæg] ælmihtig God
> nīða [generian], se ðe in nīedum īu.

See under generian in Grein's *Sprachschatz*.

1478 ff. This passage is certainly ambiguous. That **hāliges** refers to Andrew, and not to God, is shown by the use of **hē** in l. 1482.

1493. I follow Grein's emendation, and read **sælwāge** = "castle wall," although the word is not found elsewhere. If we read **sælwange** with Wülker, the meaning of **under** must be greatly stretched. Moreover, the Greek says: " He saw a pillar standing in the midst of the prison."

1508. Reading **geofon** with Grimm, Kemble, etc., as also in 393 and 1585.

1545. Reading **wadu** with Kemble and Grein.

1663. Apparently a line or two is missing here, though there is no break in the manuscript. I have translated in brackets Grein's conjectural emendation, as supplying the probable meaning.

1667. I have again translated Grein's emendation.

1681. Reading **tīrēadigra** with Kemble.

YALE STUDIES IN ENGLISH

ALBERT S. COOK, EDITOR